D1152992

Books by the same author

Art, You're Magic!
In Crack Willow Wood
Oliver Sundew, Tooth Fairy

For older readers

Flash Eddie and the Big Bad Wolf

SAM McBRATNEY

Kristal Dimond

TIMECOP

Illustrations by Martin Chatterton

WALKER BOOKS
AND SUBSIDIARIES
LONDON • BOSTON • SYDNEY

First published 1998 by
Walker Books Ltd, 87 Vauxhall Walk
London SE11 5HJ

2 4 6 8 10 9 7 5 3 1

Text © 1998 Sam McBratney
Illustrations © 1998 Martin Chatterton

The right of Sam McBratney to be identified as author of this work has been
asserted by him in accordance with the Copyright, Designs and Patents Act 1988.

This book has been typeset in Garamond.

Printed in Great Britain

British Library Cataloguing in Publication Data
A catalogue record for this book
is available from the British Library.

ISBN 0-7445-4189-1

CONTENTS

DOUBLE-TROUBLE

Hi. Kristel Dimond is the name. I'm a Timecop. I proudly wear the uniform of silver and midnight blue.

I was cruising somewhere between Jupiter and Mars when the call came through from my boss, Gusty Monroe.

9

"Get yourself back here, Dimond, we've got trouble. And when I say trouble, I mean trouble."

I turned to Lefty, my metal companion. "Sounds like a case of double-trouble, Lefty."

"Indeed it does, Inspector Dimond."
Lefty is a robot and I call him Lefty because he sits on my left.

I said, "Doesn't it bother you, Gusty, that I'm on my way to Pluto for a skiing holiday?"

It didn't bother him.

"You get back here, Dimond! Somebody has just come through a Timehole – with something that means curtains for the human race."

Naturally, I turned my patrolship around. I belong to the human race and I'm quite fond of it. "Full speed ahead, Lefty. We'd better see what's up."

THE RAINMAKER

I docked my ship on the Space
Station which orbits the Earth and
stepped into a woomzoomtube.
Lefty came too. I use him as a kind
of butler. The day before yesterday,
for example, I sent him out to Pluto
to book our skiing holiday. Lefty
doesn't get into a foul temper like
crusty old Gusty and his body is
rustproof. He skis quite well.

On the
tube I did some
thinking about
Timepirates. They
are wild characters who
nip into the future, grab some
wonderful invention, then bring it
back and sell it – before it has been
invented. This is highly dangerous
and totally illegal, of course.

14

Ever since Timeholes were
discovered, it has been against the
law to use them. We can't have
people jumping backwards and
forwards through time like
grasshoppers.
I mean,
imagine a
stone-age
lady with a
hairdrier…

When I got to Gusty he looked
ready for his pension.

"Good morning, Sir."

"Don't 'good morning' me,
Dimond, just hang out your ears
and listen. Four hundred years from
now some brainbox will invent a
device that controls
the weather, right?
No more
hurricanes,
floods or
droughts and
the Earth will
be a beautiful
garden. It's called
the Rainmaker."

16

"Hooray," I said. "What's the problem?"

"The problem is, somebody has been through Timehole Checkpoint Charlie and pinched it. He has it now. And believe me, Dimond, the weather forecast will never be the same again."

"You think he'll use it to make the weather worse?"

"Worse? He could wipe out life on Earth! He could start the next Ice Age tomorrow."

Poor old Gusty wiped his brow. I'm a cool customer myself, but even I felt warm at the thought of polar bears in my Aunty Mabel's goldfish pond. I mean, she lives just outside Blackpool.

"Dimond – we have to find this joker." And Gusty thumped the table with a hairy great fist, scattering computer disks everywhere.

ZEUS THE TETRAHEXAHEDRON

It's all very well getting grumpy and thumping tables, but where do you actually start looking for a very small needle in a haystack the size of the Universe?

You start by talking to Zeus. This is our central computer on the Space Station. Zeus is a tetrahexahedron with an IQ of about two million. No human being has beaten him at chess within living memory, but ask him can he ski and the silence is deafening.

I typed in the names of Blackjack Wilcox, John Silver and Lucinda Montcrieff – three of the all-time-great Timepirates. If anyone had the Rainmaker, it must be one of those three.

However, according to Zeus, one was in jail and the other two were missing-presumed-dead. It's a risky business going through Timeholes because you can only see them as you approach the speed of light. Avoid them like the plague, that's my advice.

I had to think, so I went back to
my ship and took off for the Milky
Way. Now and then I zapped an
asteroid with a laser torpedo. I find
this helps me to concentrate.

A thought came to me. "Suppose we wanted to go through Checkpoint Charlie, Lefty. Could the ship's computers steer us through?"

"It would be risky, Ma'am. The calculations are very complex. Only Zeus could plot a safe course through that particular Timehole."

I knew what Lefty meant. Make one mistake going into a Timehole and you pop out the other side like a bit of burned toast. That's why the pirates end up either very rich or very dead. And Checkpoint Charlie is the deadliest of all.

I buzzed Gusty on the Visiphone. "Just a thought, Sir. If our thief used Zeus to get in and out of Checkpoint Charlie, which seems likely, then Zeus must know who he is. Zeus won't give you the time of day unless you enter your personal code."

"I'll check that out, Dimond. And by the way, you might like to know that the beginning of the end has started."

"Explain please, Sir."

"The polar ice-caps are melting back on Earth. Sea-levels will be rising within hours. Do you know what this means, Dimond?"

I sure did. Goodbye, Blackpool
beach. In fact, it meant goodbye,
Blackpool.

"I'm on my way," I said.

YOU'RE UNDER ARREST, DIMOND

Two guards met me when I
returned to the Space Station. They
took my strobe-guns and said,
"You're under arrest, Dimond."

There must have been some sort of mistake, I reckoned. When we arrived at the conference room I saw Gusty, my boss. And his boss, the Commander of the Space Station. Believe me, there were a lot of brass buttons in that room.

Gusty glared at me. "I checked with Zeus like you said, Dimond. The day before yesterday someone did something very naughty. Someone asked Zeus for the co-ordinates of Timehole Checkpoint Charlie. Guess who."

I didn't have to guess. The finger of suspicion was pointing straight at Yours Truly. I shook my head.

"Are you calling Zeus a liar, Dimond?" roared the Station Commander, who has a face like a purple onion at the best of times.

"Zeus can't lie and he can't make mistakes. You used your personal code to plot a course through a Timehole, and if there's one thing I can't stand it's a crooked cop!"

All the while I was thinking: somebody has used my code to get at Zeus. But who? Nobody knew it but the people in this room. And Lefty, of course. Down below, on Earth, the ice was melting and the

water was rising and they were blaming it all on me! All of a sudden I wished I'd taken that quiet job in the Bank of Mars.

"Gusty, this is ridiculous!" I cried out with passion. "It was me who told you to check out Zeus in the first place. I've been framed – maybe by somebody in this very room!"

"That's what I told them, Dimond,"
nodded Gusty. "You're my best
officer and I trust you completely."

Sweet, loyal, ugly old Gusty – I
could almost have kissed him. But
he hadn't finished.

"That's why you have just volunteered to go through a Timehole and talk to the folks in the future. We need their help to get the Rainmaker back. Or there won't be a future – unless you happen to be a fish. Or a machine."

Hokey-pokey, hold your horses here! I mean, I'd never actually been through a Timehole. Those things scare the pants off me.

Gusty, can't we talk this over?

"You leave in ten minutes or we stick you in jail," said the Station Commander. I have never been fond of that man.

THROUGH A TIMEHOLE

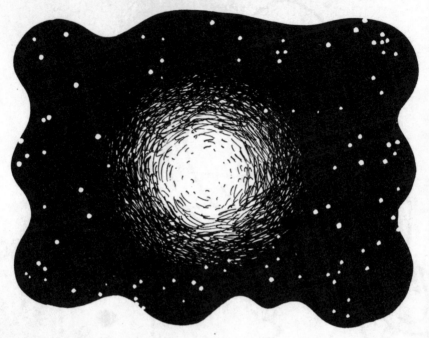

It looked like a round shimmer of light, the entrance to a kaleidoscope hanging in interstellar space. Just staring at that Timehole made the butterflies in my stomach feel more like ferrets.

I didn't want to go. All of a sudden, jail seemed like my idea of paradise. At least I'd live to come out again.

A message came up on my screen:

Do not be alarmed.
We have control of
your craft.
We will bring you
through the Timehole.

I just had time to wonder who "we" might be before the kaleidoscope rushed at me and I was going through.

What a trip! This is one ride they don't have at Disneyland. My blood seemed to boil and set my veins on fire while my poor heart went crazy.

When I dared to look I saw my
ship was sinking as slowly as a
bubble towards a great city which
sparkled like crystals in the middle
of an ocean blue.

Ye gods and stars, I thought, I'm in the future! Old Gusty has been dead for four or five hundred years and maybe so have I. Believe me, this is the kind of thinking that gives you goosepimples.

My ship stopped sinking. I was
hanging there, suspended in time
and space above the crystal city,
when a voice spoke inside my head
– a soft voice, like a whisper:

"We understand the problem, Inspector Dimond. We are returning you to your own time with a device to help you find the Rainmaker, and destroy it. You must also destroy the device we shall give you. Goodbye."

Hokey-pokey, we hadn't even said hello! "Don't I get to meet anybody?" I asked.

Let's face it, I was curious. Were they the same as us? Did human beings still have chins? Were they ten foot tall? What was everybody wearing?

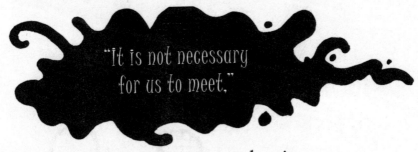

"It is not necessary for us to meet,"

said the voice in my brain.
Perhaps they didn't trust my
ancient germs.

"But what happens if I fail or
something? I'm no superwoman,
you know."

"You will not fail."

And that was that. The voice within
my head faded away as I
boomeranged back through the
Timehole. The fate of Blackpool,
not to mention the entire human
race, depended on Yours Truly.

EXIT STAGE LEFT

They had given me a Mindprobe.
All I had to do was point this little
thing the size of my fist at people
and it read their minds. It told me
what they were thinking. Lying was
impossible.

When I got back to the Space Station, I pointed the Mindprobe at everybody from the Station Commander down to the tea-boy, and you wouldn't believe what goes on inside the heads of some people!

I even scanned old Lefty, but all I got was a buzz. His brain runs on batteries, after all.

"Well?" said Gusty. He sounded
desperate. News had come from
Earth that the North Pole was
shrinking and an iceberg bigger
than the Rock of Gibraltar had sunk
an oil-rig near Aberdeen. "Do we
know the lousy traitor or don't we?"

"Afraid not," I said. "They're all in the clear. Whoever has the Rainmaker, he's not on the Space Station, Sir."

"That's it then," wailed Gusty.

There's nothing we can do!

But some things were bothering me. Who had access to Zeus? Who knew me well enough to use my code? Who was capable of fooling the Mindprobe? And above all, who didn't give two hoots about the human race or what happened to it?

What I needed now were some moments of pure thought to add up two plus two and come up with the answer four. I climbed into my ship and pointed its nose at Ursa Major.

And then I knew. Call it intuition, call it genius, call it whatever you like – I had a moment of clear-seeing.

AIRLOCK

I said, "Lefty, check the airlock for me, there's a good chap."

"Of course, Ma'am," purred Lefty.

Once he was in the airlock, I sealed it. There was no way back unless I let him out again.

"Lefty, repeat my personal code –
the one I use for communicating
with Zeus."

"By all
means. Your
code is
05KD661X."

"Thank
you."

"My aim is
always to
please,
Ma'am."

"Is it? But it's my guess that you used my code and hopped through time, Lefty. You're the joker we've been looking for all along. And the Rainmaker must be on Pluto, where you went to book our skiing holiday. You may correct me if I'm wrong."

There was a pause. "Your thinking is correct, Ma'am."

"One more thing, Lefty. I know how you did it and when you did it. But why? That's the part I can't figure out."

"It is simply a matter of change, Inspector Dimond. Human beings were not the first form of life on Earth and they will not be the last. Once dinosaurs ruled the planet and now there are none. The time of the thinking electronic being has come."

"The smart machine, eh?"

"Correct. We are stronger than you. Humans grow old and die and you make errors. Therefore the future is ours. As you say – it is the time of the smart machine."

I pressed EJECT and emptied the airlock.

"The Daleks tried it too, my metal friend. Exit stage left, near the Great Bear."

I set a course for Pluto. Maybe I should have blasted old Lefty with my lasers, but I didn't have the heart. He's out there somewhere.

Maybe his batteries are still running and he thinks about me the odd time.

Goodbye, Lefty.
And hello, Blackpool.